RABBIT STEW

A Grosset & Dunlap **ALL ABOARD BOOK**®

For my son, Tristan—D.K.

To Mom & Dad & Lisa with love—T.P.

 Published by Grosset & Dunlap, Inc., a member of Penguin Putnam Books for Young Readers, New York. GROSSET & DUNLAP is a trademark of Grosset & Dunlap, Inc. ALL ABOARD BOOKS is a trademark of Grosset & Dunlap, Inc. Registered in the U.S. Patent and Trademark Office. THE LITTLE ENGINE THAT COULD and engine design are trademarks of Platt & Munk, Publishers, a division of Grosset & Dunlap, Inc. Published simultaneously in Canada. Printed in the U.S.A.

Library of Congress Cataloging-in-Publication Data

Kosow, Donna.

Rabbit stew / by Donna Kosow ; illustrated by Tamara Petrosino.

p. cm.—(All aboard books)

Summary : Dog plans to make stew out of the rabbits that keep eating the vegetables in his garden, but the rabbits are too smart for him.

[1. Dogs—Fiction. 2. Rabbits—Fiction 3. Cookery—Fiction.]

[I. Petrosino, Tamara, ill. II. Title. III. Series : Grosset & Dunlap all aboard books.

PZ7.K85275Rab 1999

[E]—dc21

98-36357

CIP

AC

ISBN 0-448-41493-7 A B C D E F G H I J

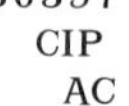

Rabbit Stew

By Donna Kosow
Illustrated by Tamara Petrosino

Grosset & Dunlap, Publishers

Once, a while back, in a rickety old shack, there lived a dog. He wasn't very smart, he didn't have much money, but he was happy. The dog had a garden, laid out in neat rows, nestled in a sunny meadow.

SEEDS

In the spring, the dog planted seeds in his garden. In the summer, he cared for the plants and watched them grow. Then he would pick and eat the vegetables he'd grown. The dog loved his garden.

But he had one big problem. Hungry rabbits would sneak into his garden and nibble on his vegetables.

They made holes in his cabbage leaves.

They dug up his carrots and potatoes.

And they chewed on his parsley.

The dog tried chasing the rabbits away, but they always came back.

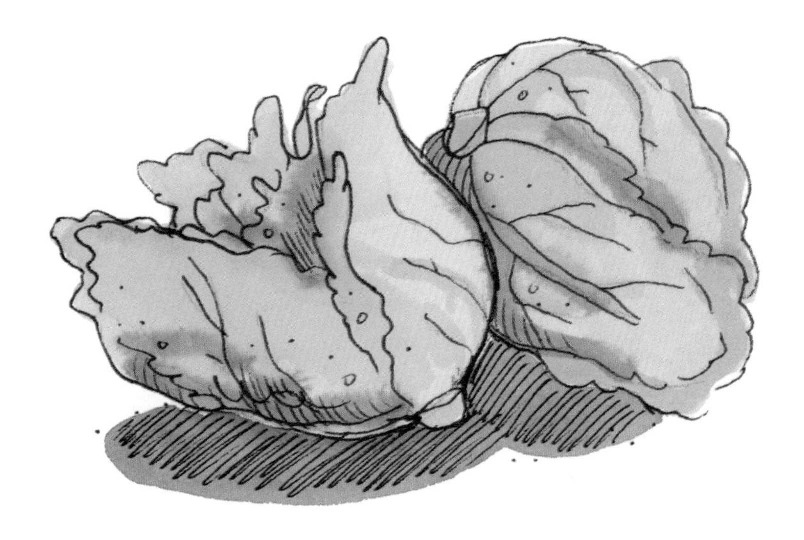

Then one day the dog looked out his window and saw those darn rabbits eating all his tender new lettuce plants. That was the last straw. The dog ran into the garden and chased the rabbits around and around until he caught them at last with a leap and a pounce.

"Hmm," thought the dog. "Now, what should I do with these pesky rabbits? Maybe I'll make a rabbit stew. Yes, I think that's what I'll do."

So the dog took the rabbits inside and put them in a large cooking pot. Then he opened his cookbook. But he couldn't find a recipe for rabbit stew, and he didn't know what to do.

FOOD
SOUPS
HERBS
Cooking

One clever rabbit said, "You could go out to the garden and get some carrots to put in the stew."

"Good idea," thought the dog. So he said to the little rabbits, "Wait right here while I go out to the garden to get some carrots."

And the little rabbits nodded their heads and said, "Oh yes, oh yes. We'll try our best."

Cooking

But as soon as the dog went out to the garden, the rabbits leaped from the pot and scampered happily out the door. When the dog returned, he saw that all the rabbits were gone. He dropped the carrots into the pot, feeling a little disappointed.

The next day, when the dog looked out his window, the rabbits were nibbling on his onions.

So the dog chased them around and around until he caught them at last with a leap and a pounce. Then he took those rabbits back inside and put them back in the large cooking pot.

"Now," said the dog, "I have rabbits and carrots to make rabbit stew."

Then one little rabbit said, "But you must have celery for rabbit stew."

"You're sure?" said the dog. "I'll go out to the garden to get some celery. But this time you have to remember to stay in the pot. Okay?"

The little rabbits nodded their heads and said, "Oh yes, oh yes. We'll try our best."

S
P

But as soon as the dog went out to the garden, all the rabbits scampered happily out the door.

When the dog came back, he saw that the rabbits were gone. As he put the celery in the pot, he thought to himself, "Those rabbits aren't very smart. They forgot to stay in the pot again."

The next day, the hungry rabbits sneaked into the garden again. So the dog chased them around and around until he caught them at last with a leap and a pounce. Then he put those rabbits back in the large cooking pot.

"I have rabbits and carrots and celery," said the dog. "Now I can make rabbit stew."

"But you must have potatoes and onions to make rabbit stew," said one clever rabbit.

"Yes, I know," said the dog, trying to look smart. "But if I go out to the garden, you rabbits will forget to stay in the pot."

After thinking a bit, one rabbit said, "You could shut the door. Then we couldn't run out that way."

"Good idea," thought the dog. Then he said to the rabbits, "Now, you stay in the pot while I go dig up some potatoes and onions."

The rabbits nodded their heads and said, "Oh yes, oh yes. We'll try our best."

Out to the garden the dog went, closing the door behind him. As soon as he was gone, the rabbits leaped to the window and jumped out. Then away they ran, glad they had fooled the dog again.

When the dog came back, he saw that the rabbits were gone. He put the potatoes and onions in the pot, and to his surprise, the pot was full to the top with vegetables. There was no room for rabbits.

"It's just as well that the rabbits are gone," said the dog, "because they wouldn't fit in the pot anyway. I'll just make rabbit stew without the rabbits." Then he felt very proud for having such a good idea.

Happily, the dog poured some water into the pot, turned on the stove, and cooked his "rabbit stew." It smelled delicious.

For supper he ate three big bowls of stew. Then, when he couldn't eat another bite, the dog put some of the leftover stew outside for the rabbits. "After all," he said to himself, "those rabbits might not be very smart, but they sure know how to make a good rabbit stew."